BLUFF YOUR WAY IN MUSIC

Russell Robinson
Peter Gammond

CENTENNIAL PRESS

ISBN 0-8220-2213-3
U.S. edition © Copyright 1989 by Centennial Press
British edition © Copyright 1985 by The Bluffer's Guides

Printed in U.S.A.
All Rights Reserved

Centennial Press, Box 82087, Lincoln, Nebraska 68501
an imprint of Cliffs Notes, Inc.

INTRODUCTION

At least 98 percent of most Americans used to listen to "good music" (as opposed to "bad music") against their will for at least part of their childhood, such as those dismal Sunday afternoons when Great-Aunt Lucibelle (the one with the estate in Connecticut) came to call. However, only a minuscule number of the 98 percent cared about the technicalities or the murky, convoluted history of music (except for the racier parts, like those hinted at in Columbia's *A Song to Remember,* a 1945 movie about Chopin and the androgynous George Sand).

This book isn't written with the surreptitious intention of dispersing a wealth of knowledge to bolster games of Trivial Pursuit or prepare the reader for *Jeopardy.* Au contraire. The way to prosper, as all good bluffers know, is to possess a minimum number of facts and stretch them over a maximum number of situations, carefully placing tidbits of knowledge alongside profound pauses, knowing glances, and appropriate gestures—depending on the depth of one's adversary. Nor is this valuable guide written, as is most musical criticism, for critics and experts. They already know the tricks of the trade and don't need help from the likes of us.

To be comfy with a vast and complicated subject like music, the average person (which no one *ever* claims to be) doesn't need to memorize dates or the arcane ins and outs of musical theory (although anyone who wishes to do so may go right ahead and learn it all). To render an appearance of ease with the subject, this book is all you'll need. It goes quietly behind the mysteries of music and, with tact and a modicum of taste, exposes them. Absorb its discreet, but incisive message, and you'll master the first steps from innocence and dilettantism toward expert bluffery.

THE GENTLE ART

It's common knowledge that music consists of an indiscriminate mix of melody, harmony, and rhythm, all of which most people enjoy in one form or other. Primarily, music *drugs* the listener. More world-weary individuals prefer amphetamines, booze, cigarettes, CDs (certificates of deposit, not the other kind), steamy novels, or the Hallelujah Corner to escape today's ennui and/or stress. Music has a similar effect and hurts nobody (except the poor soul on the other side of the condo wall from your quadraphonic system while you play *Victory at Sea*, the *1812 Overture*, or that sword-of-Gideon section of Wagner that ignites the helicopter attack in *Apocalypse Now*).

Little of the music which we listen to today is played by professional gentlemen in tuxes and ladies in black crepe de Chine in overheated auditoriums. The majority of contemporary "music" pours out of radios, televisions, stereos, loudspeakers, and tiny plugs imbedded in skateboarders' ears. Laundromat-goers, armed with an Everest of wash, usually face the challenge with the help of their favorite easy-listening station. Teenagers work off pent-up frustrations by rending the peace with ear-splitting boom boxes or driving cars that sound like mobile rock concerts. Motorists cope with the tedium of freeway-turned-parking-lot by tuning in anything at hand. Diners chew and swallow to the Muzak that wafts across the dining room, adjusting their metabolism to whatever pleases the maître d'. The average person – burned out by high taxes, aerobic fallout, and general malaise – goes home and gazes into space while music oozes from home speakers and soothes the gastric wake of a couple of Jack Daniels.

In this sense, music serves a definite purpose: it probably saves many people who are at the brink of insanity and stops the hand that fingers the trigger of the AK-47 or the pin of a grenade. Who knows – without music, we all might be fighting minor engagements or border skirmishes instead of pounding the 88s or singing *The Impossible Dream* in the shower.

Don't be fooled, though, into surmising that music exists simply for human "enjoyment." Actually, it's long held an enviable place among the arts. To wear the label of "art," nothing can serve as "mere pleasure." Indeed, art is a by-product of that general symptom of human decline called civilization.

Enjoyable pastimes become "art" once *money* is involved. The first Zamfir who carved holes into a section of bamboo to amuse kids with simple tunes on a rainy afternoon never knew what he was starting. In fact, it seems likely that the first *professional* musician was the court reed-pipist in some moldy Mesopotamian palace – and chances are, the pipist received heavy criticism in the daily newspapyrus and may even have been beheaded as a result of an overly persnickety critic.

Some arts – music, for example – give employment to a mass of people, and someone is bound to garner the goodies. The only question is, *which* artist will get the crown? Once you accept cash, you open yourself to criticism. Then some clever smarties will manage to get paid for doing the criticizing. Of course, they in turn lay themselves directly in the path of other critics. And so it goes. *Every*body's a critic.

Instead of music remaining an unassuming accompaniment for foot- and finger-tapping, it becomes a talking (or arguing) point. The whole idea of discussing anything is to put the know-it-alls in their places. If you can quote chapter and verse from Grove's *Dictionary of Music and Musicians,* you can easily squelch any newcomer on the bluffing scene. Very few bluffers, however, have the time or inclination to go to such lengths.

Thus, we humbly suggest shortcuts.

THE HISTORY OF MUSIC

It's extremely important to get your sense of chronology right. To begin with, we can wipe the slate clean of most early music – obliterating plainsong, Gregorian chant, Palestrina, and other minutiae – and focus on the last part of the seventeenth century, when music really got to be *music.* The main eras in their chronological order of importance include:

Baroque
Classical
Romantic
Impressionistic
Modern

This book will cover each era in turn. Secretly we believe that composers outrank individual periods and performers, but composers are notoriously difficult to interview – expecially if they're dead. Nonetheless, we'll devote lots of space to them under each subhead. There's no reason why we shouldn't set a precedent.

The Baroque Era (1685–1750)

When people think of the **baroque era**, they tend to envision naked cherubs in gold leaf, gracing sconces and frames and other emblems of richness and singularity. This is baroque, and the musical world began the era by departing from the dull, predictable music that was being composed in Italy. **Claudio Monteverdi** (1567–1643) started dabbling in musical alterations and inventions, and **Antonio Vivaldi** (1678–1741) assembled an all-girl orchestra. France, not to be left out of new twists on an old theme, produced some ballets and operas of note, but no particular paragon. The English put **Henry Purcell** (1659–95) on the bandwagon as Restoration music began emulating French and Italian models in order to bring some pizzazz to stuffy London concert halls.

But the great redoers of musical taste – the Germans – spawned **Johann Sebastian Bach** (1685–1750), whose organ solos, cantatas, motets, oratorios, and dramatic passions left other nationals in the dust. Most would-be musicians approach the great master with rubber knees. Bach isn't merely a musical commodity – he's a religion. Adored by intellectual virgins, Bach's music is a pseudo-substitute for sex (depending on how much you're willing to forgo to attain the sublime). Its purity grips minds which are, by nature, too rarified for the trappings of proper religion. Bach's canon should be admired, sung, played, and discussed with an expression of ineluctable piety. Compared with him, Beethoven and Mozart come off as poor seconds, maybe even thirds.

It's possible to like Bach and no one else – it's even likely. In spite of the clinical and demanding nature of his music, it remains tremendously popular. If you meet a real Bach groupie, you make a lasting impression by fainting – or, at least, feigning unending rapture. Any suggestion that you can take Bach or leave him will earn you a sullied reputation, possibly even scorn. With Bach, you take him *sehr* seriously – or not at all. There's no middle.

Fortunately, a single, sincere gasp of "Ahhh, Bachhh!" nets you high marks for taste and discrimination. We realize that this ploy is rather thin, but if you stick to this one remark and vary your inflection, you can cover all bases and navigate a safe course in the treacherous waters inhabited by aficionados.

One can feel sorry for Bach, privately, because he reputedly fathered twenty children. There's not much that you can add in a critical spirit about his life. As a youth, he walked over 200 miles to hear Buxtehude play the organ. Not even standing through a midnight rendering of the *Messiah* can equal that for musical devotion. After this initial penance, he settled down to a toilsome life at the keyboard, where he wrote an unremitting flood of scores, all of them clever and clean. He also raised eleven children (gossips don't account for the disparity). What else can one say about such a man except "Ahhh, Bachhh!"

Those trying to bluff Bachmania should have some knowledge of his solid golds: the six *Brandenburg Concertos,* the *2- and 3-Part Inventions* (which he wrote to educate his children), the *Passion According to St. Matthew,* and his *Mass in B Minor.* Any one of them will fill you in on the reason for nonstop Bach adulation from most of the civilized world. For the astute bluffer, it might pay to memorize a few chunks of trivia, such as the role of Albert Schweitzer in developing Bach's style on updated organs. (Don't overdo this tidbit; a simple reference along with raised eyebrows suffices. With Bach, subtlety vastly outranks overkill.)

If, by chance, you're in the company of Italians, you'll

find them loath to abandon the aforementioned **Antonio Vivaldi** – the *center* of the musical universe, according to them. Like Bach fans, Vivaldians praise not only the master's music, but also his devout life. They're quick to note that Bach too was a Vivaldi fan and copied the style and flavor of his concertos.

On the down side of his popularity, Vivaldi, according to a less-than-sycophantic critic, spent his life writing the same concerto six hundred times. This is a malicious exaggeration – he wrote four hundred and fifty (and he often took the trouble to change the solo instrument). In addition, Vivaldi wrote over forty operas, now rarely heard; of course it's possible that they're the same opera under forty different titles. Even one of his leading supporters has described them as "written in haste and confusion and full of waste material." So much for longevity.

Only Vivaldi's *Four Seasons* has attained real success. If you're not familiar with this work, check out the Alan Alda movie of the same title. The background music for the film is pure Vivaldi. A carefully cultivated admiration for Vivaldi serves the bluffer well. Who's going to question a casual reference to P. 275 or P. 374 – or any of the other four hundred and forty-eight Ps, for that matter?

For the daring, a cautious insistence on the perfection of the *Gloria,* with its rich contralto solo gracing the "Domine Deus," can stand the bluffer in good stead, particularly among choral music buffs. But back off before the going gets too rough, for choral whizzes know their stuff and won't let an idle comment lie unkicked.

Another route for bluffing your way through the

baroque era avoids both Vivaldi and Bach altogether and branches out into the compositions of **George Frederic Handel** (1685-1759). Handel kindly left behind him some *Water Music* (eternally useful for all aquatic occasions), some *Royal Fireworks Music* (for pyrotechnic displays of any kind), and the *Messiah* (for regular occasions when choral societies want to raise an audience – and enough funds for new choir robes).

In spite of these gems, we ungratefully complain that Handel dominated English music for so long that he almost made the native breed of composer extinct. It was only Britten, Vaughn Williams, Elgar, and "Land of Hope and Glory" that centuries later eventually saved the situation.

If you feel the urge to prove yourself a devotee, cite lesser Handelian treasures, particularly *Ode to St. Cecilia's Day, Samson, Judas Maccabaeus,* and *Guilio Cesare* (which is Italian for "Julius Caesar," but deserves the proper fillip on *chay' ser ay* if you're bluffing it for all you're worth.)

The Classical Era (1750–1820)

All good things, even baroque music, must come to an end when a new passion finagles its way into vogue. The baroque era's twining, vine-like melodies eventually became thorny, overgrown rococo foliage. Music almost fatally constipated itself with trills, turns, and appoggiaturas. Fortunately for musicians, the pristine clarity of the **classical era** finally poured forth – like a double dose of distilled Baden Baden tonic.

"Classical" is a loose term, one that deserves assiduous tightening. Unfortunately it's usually applied to anything that's not "popular." Strictly speaking, the term "classical" should be used when referring to symphonies, concerti, sonatas, fugues, and suites composed between 1750 and 1820. For the bluffer searching for the right adjectives to throw in at appropriate moments, some useful "classical" terms are *restraint, simplicity,* and *balance.* The biggie, of course, is *form,* which opens endless horizons of conjecture and argument. (On second thought, better leave *form* to experts and stick with simple openers.)

Varying from the instrumentation of the baroque era, which was primarily strings of differentiated *timbre* (see Glossary), the high point of the classical revolt was led by **Carl Philipp Emanuel Bach** (1714–88), who brought the head count of the orchestra to two flutes, two oboes, two bassoons, two horns, two kettledrums, first and second violins, violas, cellos, and double-basses—but no harpsichord. (By the time of Haydn, Mozart, and Beethoven, the possibilities for different instrumental sections were endless, and the orchestra itself became a supple, malleable instrument, much like the voice in the great choral age.) Carl Philipp Emanuel's *Symphony in D Major* is, in a word, "unparalleled." Remember that word.

Another safe bet in any bluff of classical expertise is **Wolfgang Amadeus Mozart** (1756–91), the boy wonder who had the unique distinction of writing *koechels* (properly pronounced *kir' kelz*) instead of opuses, a feat no other composer has done before or since. Mozart's great popularity dates from the time that this absorbing fact was discovered, by some strange coincidence, by a man named Köchel.

These numbers add a wonderful air of mystery to

his works, but, as might be expected, they can be quite hazardous if not handled properly. Although no one is expected to cite Beethoven's opus numbers and would be buttoned into a white jacket with the sleeves in back if they knew all of Bach's BWV numbers, it *is* wise for the bluffer to become conversant with a few *koechels*. People have certified themselves as experts solely on off-the-cuff comparisons of K. 375b with K. 375c. It's fairly safe to do this sort of thing as the odds are pretty high against any bluffer-come-lately contradicting you. (But above all, say "koechel" 375b – never "K." 375b.) Among the koechels that you *must* know is K. 525; it's a sad affliction to have to go around referring to the *Eine Kleine Nachtmusik*. In a pinch, however, you can get away with calling it "Serenade No. 13."

You should also know K. 385, the *Haffner* Symphony; K. 425, the *Linz*; K. 504, the *Prague*; and K. 551, the *Jupiter*. You could also try to remember what K. 100, K. 200, K. 300, K. 400, and K. 500 are, but this stratagem is rather obvious. A good koechel to cite is K. 365, which is the *E-flat Concerto for Two Pianos,* – 365 being, you may remember, the number of days in an average year. People *never* refer to Mozart's *Piano Concerto No. 23* unless they want to be labeled an old fogey. If you can't remember that it's K. 488, then refer to it as "the" *A Major Concerto*. The fact that there are others in A Major leaves your opponent in an uneasy state and even more confused – especially if you say "the" instead of *the*. (Note: be careful of a trap. Don't ever discuss *Symphony No. 34*; reputedly Mozart got somebody else to write it for him because he was feeling a little off-color that day.)

A few other hot koechels to cite are K. 297b, the *E-flat*

Sinfonia Concertante; K. 622, the *Clarinet Concerto* (another number in A Major); and K. 264, which is nine piano variations on "Lison Dormait." You'll probably acquire some obscure favorites of your own if you belong to the Musical Heritage Society, a heaven on earth for devotees of obscure koechels.

You may think that we exaggerate the importance of this number business. There is, however, little else that you can bluff about concerning Mozart, for everything he wrote is perfect — with never a wrong note in it. The proper reaction to Mozart is a glassy-eyed stare and inexpressible admiration.

However, if you personally find Mozart's music as boring as the tick of a metronome, keep your handicap to yourself. You might as well say that you kick small dogs or can't see any point to the Super Bowl.

One of the most pleasing points about Mozart is that hardly anyone can perform his music well. Conductors who becalm us with Beethoven, woo us with Wagner, and beguile us with Bartók, get so nervous performing Mozart that you can count on 95 percent of their renditions being unsatisfactory. Don't *ever* hesitate to say so. As the ideal seems to be an orchestra of angels with St. Peter conducting and Mozart himself playing glockenspiel, it's quite clear why mere mortals so often fall short.

Useful, offbeat Mozart works that you might keep up your sleeve include the ballet music *Les Petits Riens*, K. 299b; *Sinfonia Concertante in E-flat for Violin and Viola*, K. 364; the *Bassoon Concerto*, K. 191; the *Wind Quintet*, K. 452; *Serenade No. 10 for 13 Wind Instruments*, K. 361; *Serenade No. 4 in D*, K. 203; and the song "Moto di Gioia," K. 579 — plus a minuet or two that's easy for you to remember. For a special treat, find a recording of K. 522, Mozart's "Musikalischer Spass" (Musical Joke). This is a *must*—and you'll see why after you listen to it.

Mozart was a randy fellow, as you might recall if you saw *Amadeus*. He was a gross-mouthed proletarian—always in hot water with various relatives and always overdrawn on his MasterCard. How much nearer perfection can a composer get?

Now, for the sake of variety after this Mozartiana, you might launch into a challenging, thought-provoking commentary on **Franz Joseph Háydn** (1732–1809), the Austrian "father" of the symphony. (Contrary to the usual pattern of things, no one knows who the "mother" was.) Modeling his thoughts after Aristotle's advice in the *Poetics,* Haydn decided that symphonies should possess a beginning, a middle, and an end. Beethoven, churlish to the end, pooh-poohed Haydn's dictum and spoiled this neat convention.

The general feeling is that Haydn could have been as good as Mozart if he hadn't been so incurably *happy.* This spirit of contentment slopped over into his music and seriously diluted it. Then he wrote (a blessing in disguise, really) his last few symphonies in London for *pounds per note.* The cloud of his "selling out" apparently hung over him and added a dramatic coloring of misery and *angst* that had been lacking before. His Symphony No. 104 is stark and commanding, filled with dark shadows—proof that Haydn had a passionate heart beneath his spotless cambric jerkin.

There's lots of virtually unplayed Haydn symphonies that you can claim as favorites, but the best recourse is to comment ominously (rather than specifically) about "superficiality muddling the best of prodigies." The less support for that statement, the better. If you're in a whimsical mood, cast doubt on Haydn's sanity by querying whether any "serious" musician would ever name any of his compositions *The Lark, The Bear, The Hen, The Queen, The Clock, The Drumroll,* – or *The Surprise,* which every six-year-old piano student can play from memory. If you need more potent ammunition, ponder the relationship between Haydn's *Creation* and Milton's *Paradise Lost.*

Now, with soup and salad under your belt, proceed to the main course: **Ludwig van Beethoven** (1770–1827). There's four composers who dwell in Valhalla, beyond the slings and arrows of outrageous criticism – Mozart, Bach, Beethoven, and your own favorite. To attempt to criticize one of these would be as fruitless as saying that Shakespeare was a poor dramatist or that you can't see why people make such a fuss about the Beatles.

There's no need to say that you "admire" Beethoven – everyone assumes as much. (You'll notice, incidentally, that no callow critic ever mentions Beethoven or Mozart – if possible. Too dangerous.) Beethoven is regarded as a public company in which the known world owns shares, and it's important to note how many shares each holds. Thus one talks of Klemperer's Beethoven, von Karajan's Beethoven, Solti's Beethoven, Bernstein's Beethoven, Toscanini's Beethoven, and, after a bit of research, Fürtwangler's Beethoven – those are the major shareholders, with Klemperer holding all the aces. Most conductors have an inner compulsion to record a complete cycle of Beethoven's symphonies. Some achieve it, but most get stuck halfway.

The only fruitful line of discussion about Beethoven is with regard to the comparative merits of the symphonies. The concerti *rarely* rate mention, especially the *Emperor* and the *Violin Concerto*, because both of them are perfect and popular and lead a conversation nowhere.

The symphony above criticism is the third, the *Eroica*. It's ineffably great but should be avoided at live concerts because it tends to become ineffably long and consequently boring. However, one shouldn't blame the *Eroica*, but content oneself with snide remarks about the *shambles* that the conductor in question made of this masterpiece.

The fifth and sixth symphonies have both risen too high in public esteem. Most people can actually hum melodies from them after only a brief warmup. The ninth, the *Choral*, is dangerous turf. Best steer the conversation away from it; no one, apart from Vaughan Williams, has concluded anything about the ninth. It's likely to raise conjecture to a serious plane, and such musings might lead to the well-established fallacy that Beethoven couldn't compose for the voice. At this point, you might discover that you're at sea in a murky discussion about *Fidelio* and the choral works.

All in all, the bluffer can be condescendingly affectionate toward Beethoven's symphonies, especially No. 1 and No. 2 (the latter is usually overlooked and it's a delightful work). The "fashionable" symphonies usually include 4, 7, and 8, although 8 is almost too good to be true. Odd-numbered symphonies of Beethoven have always been a little *over*-admired. It says much for 7's strength of character that it remains slightly less loved than 3, 5, or 9. Go for it in a big way.

The really serious Beethovenist will refer reverently to the piano sonatas. Long ago, Artur Schnabel defined them forever, and anyone who deviates from his interpretations is slightly suspect. The efforts of such poachers on these hallowed preserves as Ashkenazy, Brendel, Barenboim, or Arrau must be treated, therefore, as plus or minus so many degrees Schnabel.

The quartets on the other hand are another matter, and you have *every* right to be very severe with any comer who attempts to sound knowledgeable about them. Dry, serious discussion of the quartets should be left to *experts*. No bluffing here.

Useful items to trot out in terms of casual and affectionate familiarity include a couple of romances for violin and orchestra: *No. 1 in G*, Op. 40, and *No. 2 in F*, Op. 50. The *Septet for Nine Winds in E-flat*, Op. 20 is a real charmer, as is the *Quintet for Piano and Winds in E-flat*, Op. 16. A passing acquaintance with his notebooks also makes a good impression.

The Romantic Era (1820–1900)

Every bluffer needs a haven in which to kick back, cruise easy, and let the good times roll. Fortunately for music lovers, the **romantic era** provides safe waters. Beginning and ending with the nineteenth century (one of the easier sets of numbers to deposit into one's memory banks), the romantic era sets a dizzying course amid moonlit forests, enchanted castles, shadowy dungeons, vindictive dragons, and rutting fauns. But that's not all. This era also included an offshoot of nationalism, a revolt against convention, and a freedom of restraint that does the soul good. The delineation of the era offers some good bluffing for those who wish to carry the Beethoven crusade into the enclave of the romantics. Whatever your opinion, you're on safe ground. Bluff away.

Some significant names to drop are **Sibelius**, **Schubert**, **Grieg**, **Brahms**, **Mendelssohn**, **Chopin**, and the **Schumann**s. (To establish yourself as a *real* music buff, let people wonder who the *other* Schumann was. Then hop on the topic of repressed feminists, dividing your spoils into two camps – music *and* women's rights. It'll be a double-header and a great day for the Irish!)

Johannes Brahms (1833–97) makes a safe opener. He's a German you can't help but like – even if some of his music sounds as unutterably cluttered as a Black Forest cuckoo clock. Brahms was a cushiony fat man with a bushy beard – rather like the Smith Brothers, Santa Claus, or a full-bearded Colonel Sanders. He often conducted with one hand in his pocket – jingling change that he received in tips. It's believed that Brahms wished he had written Strauss's polkas and waltzes – then he would *really* have had coins to jingle. Supposedly he also wished he had written symphonies like Beethoven's, but whenever he set about emulating them, he got confused; the works scrolled forth and he lost count of the number of instruments he was writing for.

On the whole, Brahms led a mostly event-starved life which he brightened by being quietly rude to people and collecting tin soldiers. He was fond of Clara Schumann (the *other* Schumann), as she was of him.

It was rare for her to give a piano recital without including a work or two by Brahms. Hard-core romantics believe that after Clara died, Brahms mourned so passionately for her that he himself died a year later.

Brahms's symphonies, which seem to appeal to female admirers especially, hardly need recommendation. However, the only person who has ever really knocked them into cohesive shape was Toscanini. If you're looking for lesser known pieces to bluff with, champion Brahms's choral arrangements of German folk music, which grace many college concert programs and Biergarten bouts. If humming one of these folk tunes, throw in occasional cries of "Ja, ja" and "Bitte, bitte." Even if you don't know German, that should suffice.

Little known but doubly satisfying is Brahms's *Concerto in A Minor for Violin and Cello,* Op. 102. The *Hungarian Dances* should be admired *only in their original form*–as piano duets. For a curious, folksy pleasure in Brahms, cultivate the *Liebeslieder Waltzes,* Op. 52, a high point in romanticism.

Don't allow yourself to graze too long in Brahmsian pastures, for there's a wide array of masters of romanticism. **Franz Peter Schubert** (1797–1828), for one, suits many music lovers who weary of musical giants like Beethoven and Bach. By academic standards, Schubert was probably a bit naive and insisted on cramming melodies into nearly *everything* he wrote. He preferred clean, bouncy rhythms and accompaniments that stuck to definite patterns; he was sort of an early-nineteenth-century disco king.

But even Schubert couldn't maintain his inspiration all the time; he wrote hundreds of nondescript songs that get trotted out occasionally for recitals or recorded on Musical Heritage Society cassettes—but at least a handful of them boasts that memorable perfection which the world craves. As is evident in his oft-sung *Mass in G*, Schubert was keen on abrupt modulations into other keys, but these sound harmless by current standards, when keys are modulated by whim.

Schubert's symphonies up to No. 6 are in the Mozartian style. Then at this point, he seems to have suffered symphony burnout. He never got around to doing anything more than some preliminary sketches for No. 7 and then started No. 8 in a burst of enthusiasm, but never finished it. To make up for this slackery, he wrote an extra long and rambling 9th. On the whole, Schubert's symphonies are so endearingly simple that they suffer in performance in the way that Mozart's do. Rarely does anyone come up with a really worthwhile interpretation.

One doesn't refer to Schubert's "songs," by the way, but to his *lieder*. This is a pity because they really are songs. Lots of other people, such as Schumann, Brahms, and Strauss, wrote *lieder*, but Schubert definitely wrote "songs."

Lest you fear you'll run out of topics to spark a really fierce debate about trends in romanticism, rest assured that you have ammunition readily at hand, particularly in the area of piano solos. First, there's **Robert Schumann** (1810–56). One of his most successful works, *Carnaval,* is a series of short songs strung together like twinkling bulbs on a carousel. But beware if you're diabetic; some of his sweetie-sweet numbers may be hazardous to your health.

Less saccharine is his contemporary **Jacob Ludwig**

Felix Mendelssohn-Bartholdy (1809–47), or just plain "Mendelssohn" to his buddies. The main body of his work leans toward the classical, yet a taste for fairyland marks some of his more romantic works, particularly in the *scherzo* movements, such as the famous example in *A Midsummer Night's Dream*.

Mendelssohn's music is usually said to be "immature." He wrote all his best works when he was about seventeen – such as his famous *Octet in E-flat Major*. At the advanced age of twenty-four, he pulled himself together sufficiently to write his sparkling *Italian Symphony,* but thereafter, he managed to write only drawing room pieces for the piano and large choral works that served as models for bad Victorian music. Queen Victoria graced him with an approving smile, which was sufficient cause for condemnation by highbrow critics.

A good bluffing line concerning Mendelssohn should include a spirited defense of his piano concertos, which not many people know – especially the *double* concertos. *Definitely* keep off the *Hebrides* overture, which bears the smell of mothballs from long years of neglect. Possibly because it was Prince Albert's favorite.

One excellent trait that Mendelssohn had was his ability to give his works memorable, even metaphoric titles. The ones that stick in the mind are the *Reformation, Scottish, Italian, Elijah, Lorelei,* and *St. Paul* symphonies and the *Rondo Capriccioso.* Some of these admittedly sound a bit too romantic for words, but if you know a little German, try trotting out jawbreakers like *Lobgesang, Festgesang, Die Hochzeit des Camacho, Das Märchen von der Schönen Melusine,* and *Auf Flügeln des Gesanges.* If your German's rusty, spit these out with care, lest you throw your tongue into a double whammy and dislocate your uvula.

As a safe bet for the conclusion of any grand display of romantic expertise, any *seemingly* knowledgeable piano enthusiast can always drop back on good old **Frédéric Chopin** (1810–49). As you might already know, his life was short, alas, but it never lacked for excitement. Curiously, Chopin's music is coming back into vogue after being relegated to trifling sentimentalism by Victorian pianists. He's also gradually living down the fact that he had a bizarre affair with a cigar-smoking, trousered lady novelist (George Sand, who disdained the more characteristically feminine names of her era, such as Fanny Rose and Louisa May). You can easily spot amateur Chopin bluffers; they *rave* about his "I'm Always Chasing Rainbows" instead of acknowledging the "lyrical poignance" of his *Fantaisie-Impromptu.*

Pianists since Rubinstein (who played Chopin's music with steely fingers on hard-toned pianos with speed and brilliance) have persuaded us that Chopin is every bit as good as Liszt — if not better. Chopin himself had no doubts on the matter. He described Liszt as "a clever craftsman without a vestige of talent."

Chopin admirers usually sigh over the least unbending of his works, like the Etudes and the Preludes, but if you enjoy the Valses, Scherzos, Nocturnes, Mazurkas, and Polonaises, just say so. Surprisingly, you *may* get away with it. When cornered on matters of taste, insist that the "dissonant harmonic idiom" and "rich sonority" of Chopin's elusive fantasies "more than compensate for any other lapses." They do.

Profess admiration for the *Cello Sonata in G Minor,*

Op. 65, and a great disdain for the done-to-death *Les Sylphides,* even if you secretly enjoy it. Reverently refer to Chopin's "treasure": the *Polonaise in C for Cello and Piano,* Op. 3; insist that Chopin is *the* composer for the cello. Sure, 99 percent of Chopin's talent was devoted to piano, but you can rest easy in the knowledge that no garden variety adversary will challenge you on the other 1 percent.

If you bluffingly claimed to love "the intimacy and the agony" of Chopin, proclaim that romanticism is a many-splendored thing and trot out your fondness for his temperamental opposite: Berlioz. **Hector Berlioz** (1803–69) scares the timid bluffer and the dilettante alike because he was a consummate professional about the whole business. He knew *exactly* what he wanted from musicians and wrote large critical works which made him unpopular among critics and historians who don't like composers flaunting their literacy.

Berlioz composed music that's suitable for movie backgrounds and signature tunes that seem perfect for TV mini-series. Clearly he was in league with the devil. His *Symphonie Fantastique* is played regularly at some of the best Sabbats and bears out the fact that the devil has *all* the best tunes. You may secretly admire and even enjoy Berlioz's works and build a naughty little reputation as a musical sensualist.

To sound really smart, suggest to a casual acquaintance that he or she come over and listen to "The Royal Hunt" and "Storm" from *Les Troyens* or to *L'enfance du Christ.* If they claim to already have CDs of these works, you can always compare Berlioz's precocity with that of Haydn or Mozart. (Comparisons of apples and oranges have been quite beneficial to the reputations of most bluffers. Don't pass up a winning combination.)

Berlioz was a tremendous influence on the young French composer **Camille** (Hold on – don't jump to conclusions. "Camille," in this case, is a male) **Saint-Säens** (*san sahn*) (1835–1921), another of those musician-composers who were child prodigies. Fortunately, Saint-Säens's genius had longevity. When he was six, he was performing Mozart and Beethoven concertos in public, and a few years later, he astounded even the great Wagner by sight-reading and playing the master's formidable opera scores; when he was 86, he played a complete program of his own piano compositions for a concert in Algiers. Now *that's* longevity.

As a young man in search of a fortune, Saint-Säens first made his mark as one of Paris's best organists, in addition to composing an immense number of symphonic works – at a time when the French populace was bored sick of anything vaguely "symphonic." French music had become synonymous with "restraint, clarity, and balance," and the public was tired of their music being a cliche. They preferred ballets and operas, and it was some time before they discovered that Saint-Säens's works had the same romantic, turbulent emotions as Berlioz's compositions.

For the essence of Saint-Säens, be familiar with the *Concerto for Cello and Orchestra in A Minor*, Op. 33 (mention the "rippling triplet rhythms" of its theme and the "brilliant sonority" of the cello's "harmonics"); refer to the *Suite Algerienne* (a "luscious, exotic" tone poem); and profess a fondness for his Symphony No. 3 ("I know that they call it the "Organ" symphony, but has anyone *ever* created such magic for the *woodwinds?*"

In any discussion of Saint-Säens, *don't* mention his *Carnival of the Animals* (everyone has played "The Swan" sometime in their short-lived piano careers); nor should you refer to *Samson and Delilah*. If you do – ten to one, you'll hear whoever's listening to you begin the first bars of "My Heart at Thy Sweet Voice," which is almost as groaningly done-to-death as "We've Only Just Begun."

When enthusiasm begins to wane in your Berlioz camp, strike up the band and move along to **Richard Wagner** (1813–83), a composer who obtained the notable distinction of being stamped "unacceptable" by the newly formed state of Israel – mainly because he was so fervently embraced by Hitler's Third Reich. Outspoken about the importance of *message* in the arts, Wagner composed musical *dramas,* sculptured from the entire range of orchestral instruments. He palpated the human voices at his disposal in order to wring out startlingly emotional and dramatic scenes, notably in *Tristan and Isolde, Tannhäuser, Die Meistersinger, Lohengrin, Das Rheingold, Die Walküre,* and *Götterdammerung* (the latter three being sections of his masterful *Ring des Nibelungen*).

If that gave you Deutsche indigestion, consider bluffing with **Franz Liszt** (1811–86). Chopin sneered that Liszt was "an excellent binder who puts other people's works between the covers." Believe it. Nearly two-thirds of the prodigious amount of music that Liszt "wrote" was other people's. Liszt was a confirmed *arranger* who could profit in any age. He took other men's music (the simpler the better) and filled up the spaces with masses of black notes, thick chords, runs that hardly anyone but he could play, impossible octaves, and ridiculous leaps. He recoiled in horror when he saw a plain tune in all its nakedness and hastened to swathe it in multitudes of arpeggios. He saw all music as one eternal *cadenza* (see Glossary).

At heart, Liszt was more pianist than composer, and like all pianists, he thought the best part of a concerto was when the whole orchestra and the conductor sat quiet as nuns, hands stilled while the soloist caressed the piano like an octopus in overdrive.

In between bouts of enjoying his virtuosity and eating caviar, Liszt became disgusted with the whole racket and did penance by frittering away his money to charity, turning to religion, and steeping himself in Wagner. Then he succumbed to the urge for some high life and rushed off on yet another concert binge, forgetful that he was dressed all in black, like a mad bishop.

In his later years he became seriously religious, wrote some complicated music of his own, and became known as *Abbé Liszt*. Despite his religious leanings, his fellow composers never forgave him. It took *years* for them to get their works played in their original forms again. Critics today have finally forgiven him, however, and diagnose his case as acute scherzophrenia. However, pieces like *La Campanella* (although pinched from Paganini), *Piano Concerto in E-flat, Les Préludes,* and the *Grand Marche Chromatique* are now considered worthy offerings.

Since you're discussing Liszt — and probably bored — you might find it fun to discover precisely who's bluffing who (or "whom," if you're talking to a supposedly musically literate English major). There is available (and you might as well know about it and use it) a nonfail musical bluffer's test. The bait that you throw out the next time you're talking about Liszt is named "Czerny" (*chair' knee*). Whether you find yourself in a situation where someone is gushing about Liszt's *Hungarian Rhapsodies* or decrying the limpid sameness of his *Preludes*, comment (as though it were a commonplace), "Well, what you can *expect* from a pupil of Czerny's?"

You don't have to know one *thing* about Czerny himself. If your musical friend groans and visibly winces, cease your bluffing—chances are, she's (or he's) legit and knows all too well about one of Czerny's masterworks—a musically obscene little book entitled *The School of Fingering.* All fourth-year piano students are subjected to Czerny. He's the musical equivalent of the Japanese university exam. If you pass Czerny, you usually go on to Great Things, or at least attain a certain fame as an audition accompanist on either coast.

Carl Czerny (1791–1857) was born in Austria—and because of that fact alone, he should have been a better composer—but the fact is that he wasn't. He wrote literally thousands of piano pieces—or *etudes* (as he and Frenchified musicologists prefer to call them)—and it's no exaggeration to say that a person can take a pair of scissors and cut and paste any number of random measures together and the *etude* won't sound any more or any less melodic. Everything that Czerny wrote sounds exactly alike. One always hears about his "big, serious compositions," but no one ever records them or plays them in concert. They're sort of like musical UFOs.

One positive note about Czerny: those who passed their Czerny Endurance Finals can rest easy knowing that one of Czerny's contemporaries hoodwinked the

Master. He painted a portrait of Czerny, in which the Master is gazing druggedly out at us (his splay-fingered disciples), while ominous dark clouds tumultuously rise toward his no-neck omnipotence. And at that moment, WHAM! the subliminal message hits us—Czerny is being burned at the stake! Oh divine retribution! There's only one regret: someone neglected to toss in *The School of Fingering.*

While you're rolling, close in with a strong position on **Richard** (*ree' card*) **Strauss** (1864–1949). (Be certain that you differentiate him from **Johann Strauss, Jr.,** who wrote *hundreds* of waltzes, polkas, mazurkas, and operettas, most of which languish in the attic.) Richard probably regretted that he was not Johann (he was not even a poor second cousin once removed), and no doubt Richard wrote *Der Rosenkavalier* to prove that he *could* have been just as successful had he wanted. He was probably the most unpopular composer of his time. There are signs today, however, that Richard will probably become one of the most admired composers of all time—when he has been forgiven his great success with *The Merry Pranks of Till Eulenspiegel,* a classic which manages to be both supremely clever and enjoyable. *Violent, emotional,* and *vulgar* are words which are no longer used to describe the music of Richard Strauss. His most popular work is undoubtedly the first minute or so of *Also Spach Zarathustra,* which opens one of Elvis's in-concert albums, as well as the movie *2001.*

Nationalism

From the more individualistic expressions of romanticism evolved the struggle for freedom and the overthrow of tyranny. This genre of romanticism has its own *-ism,* known as **nationalism**, and it burst upon the European scene with the demise of the short Corsican Napoleon Bonaparte and raised folklore and the life of the commoner above even the level of court subjects. Patriotism became an acceptable reason for playing music, particularly if the notes reflected the folk culture of an identifiable people.

Marginally, the Austrian **Johann Strauss, Jr.** (1825–99), known as the "Waltz King," anticipated the more serious strains of nationalism when he elevated the concert waltz to a high plane of elegance. The son of Johann Strauss, Sr., and the brother of Josef and Eduard Strauss—Johann, Jr., evolved from a family of prolific musicmakers of the *oom-pah* variety. He used a permutatory method of composition—the constant rearrangement of groups of notes until something good materialized. Approximately one of every three of his compositions turned out to be a masterpiece. This was a very arduous method of achievement, but it was quite feasible for a dance band leader like Strauss, who presumably had lots of time on the coach between gigs. Duke Ellington and George Gershwin had a similar liking for composing while in transit, and it never did them any harm either.

Strauss, Jr.'s good waltzes—especially "The Blue Danube," "Tales from the Vienna Woods," " Voices of Spring," "The Emperor Waltz," "Pizzicato Polka," and "Artist's Life"—are *very* good and may now be mentioned in the most select musical circles without risk of condescension. Likewise, his *Die Fledermaus* and *The Gypsy Baron* are two of the most perfect operettas ever written.

But Strauss, Jr., is a lightweight when compared with the real giants of nationalistic music — **Bêdrich Smetana** (1824-84), **Peter Ilyitch Tchaikovsky** (1840-93), **Modest Petrovich Mussorgsky** (1839-81), **Antonin Dvorak** (1841-1904), **Edvard Grieg** (1843-1907), **Jean Sibelius** (1865-1957) — and **John Philip Sousa** (1854-1932), America's addition to the lineup.

Smetana, a Czechoslovakian composer and conductor from Bohemia, was the first Czech to score with the critics. A disciple of Liszt and Wagner, he suffered the disdain of Austrian critics and ran away from home to Sweden, where he established a better following — which is a good idea for any artist.

Back in Prague, he produced his lustiest work, *The Bartered Bride,* and his country hugged him to its bosom. From then on, he could do no wrong — particularly after his *Ma Vlast* (My Fatherland), which includes the popular "Moldau," dedicated to a local river, always a useful topic in nationalistic works, which are sometimes all wet.

Smetana's Russian colleague **Tchaikovsky** was born too early to write for films and thus missed a grand opportunity for enormous wealth and success. Nonetheless, even in kopek-poor Russia, his music's rich melodic vein, brilliant orchestral color, and strong emotional expression, garnered him early popularity. This wasn't enough, though, and Tchaikovsky became increasingly depressed about public acclaim, fearing that he would never be taken *seriously.* (Actually, depressed Russians are a cliche. He would have to think up a better *persona* if he were alive today.) Thus, you mustn't ever take Tchaikovsky *too* seriously. Enjoy him—warts and all. He was once married for eleven weeks but quickly saw the flaws in the institution and tried to drown himself. Recovering from a severe cold, he accepted the generous subsidy of an anonymous benefactress. He conducted symphonies in New York City, Philadelphia, and Baltimore but became homesick for his native land. Not long afterward, he died—from drinking unboiled water. (He and his music have a passionate flair for melodramatic heroics.)

All things considered, though, it's hard to trivialize Tchaikovsky's passion; one of his most passionate works contains the French national anthem, the Russian national anthem, and fully charged cannons in the background. For the sake of health and auditory safety, you'd best use due caution with the *1812 Overture*, which has been known to split speakers in the next condo and sever friendships a block away.

It's absolutely essential if you're a Tchaikovsky bluffer to find some off-the-beaten-track work which has never had and is never likely to enjoy the popularity of his *Symphonie Pathétique, The Nutcracker, Sleeping Beauty, Swan Lake, Marche Slave,* and *Romeo and Juliet.* Suggested unpopular works: *Grand Sonata in G* and the *Hamlet* overture. The first three symphonies are also interestingly dull. And long.

You might do better bluffing with Tchaikovsky's countryman **Mussorgsky**, whose fame rests on his choral-symphonic artistry. Best known for *Boris Godunov,* Mussorgsky led a nervous life, alternating between dilettante and bureaucrat after his impoverishment, following the freeing of the serfs. Under the influence of Rimsky-Korsakov, Mussorgsky solidifed his technique and moved in with the master—until Mrs.

Rimsky-Korsakov put an end to their buddy-buddy arrangement.

For supreme bluffery, avoid all mention of his *Pictures from an Exhibition* and forge right ahead into Russian never-never land. Dwell on *Sorochinsky Fair* and *Khovanshchina* for maximum effect of your musical expertise (both of these pieces are operas allegedly finished by friends). Your adversary will gladly change the subject to Humperdinck's *Hänsel and Gretel* just to get you out of expectorating any more Russian polysyllabics.

Turning to less strenuous pickings, we come to **Dvorak**, a hard-working son of a pork butcher, who looked like one himself. With a head filled with dance rhythms and country melodies, he lived amiably and wrote countless works, assigning them wrong opus numbers. He spent two years in America and actually enjoyed the experience – turning it to good account by writing his bestseller, the *New World Symphony*. Dvorak's music is so full of Bohemian atmosphere that practically all orchestras play him well, but only the Czech Philharmonic can really unlock the heart of Dvorak's music.

The only fault that one can find with Dvorak is his inordinate admiration for Brahms and Wagner (which sometimes inspired him to write their works instead of his own) and those tiresome accents on his name which printers nearly always get wrong (thus, we're ignoring them altogether).

Some special (and relatively obscure) Dvorakian delights are the *Serenade for Strings*, Op. 22; the *Scherzo Capriccioso*, Op. 66; the *Piano Quintet*, Op. 81; and the *Dumky* trio, Op. 90.

Dvorak's contemporary **Grieg** was a personable soul who wished no harm to anyone. Being very small, Grieg wrote mostly very small works – the outstanding exception being his *Piano Concerto in A Minor*, which is near the top of most classical hit parades. Before the popularity of Mozart's "Elvira Madigan," more records of this work were sold than of any other popular classic. It's imperative therefore to steer your remarks *away* from this concerto and find hidden delights in his other pieces.

The most remarkable of his compositions is the incidental music to Ibsen's weird play *Peer Gynt* – music of such dramatic unsuitability that it and the play parted company years ago. The most likeable Grieg pieces are probably the *Holberg Suite*, Op. 40, and the *Norwegian Dances*, Op. 35, preferably in their original piano duet form. Check out (but don't ever admit it) Florence Henderson (sans her Wesson bottle) in Grieg's biographical movie, *Song of Norway*; she's eons better than Julie Andrews in this genre.

Way down south of Norway, scooting under the wire just before the curtain went down on the era of romantic nationalism was the Spanish composer **Manuel de Falla** (*duh faw' yuh*) (1876–1946), who has a solid international reputation, although most Americans are hesitant to admit that they like his music. Even his innocently sin-suous (if darkly perfumed) *Three-Cornered Hat* won't pass muster if the concert audience is made up of mostly Baptists. Anything Spanish (or Mexican) is just a little too "pulsating" for our Puritan-marrowed musical tastes. So, in a word, de Falla is suspect. However, you can change your whole image by wholeheartedly bluffing that de Falla is one of Spain's—if not the world's—greatest artistic treasures.

For the fun of it, announce that once—just once—you'd like to orchestrate an orgy to de Falla's *El Amor Brujo* (*brew ho*). If some cinematic flake says, "It's been done—to the tune of Ravel's *Bolero*," smile indulgently and come back with, "Oh you *would* like that—no foreplay." *El Amor Brujo* is a rich, flashy song and dance creation centering on a ravishingly beautiful young gypsy woman, Candelas, and her attempts to exorcise the memory of her two-timing former lover. The mezzo Candelmas sings lots of gut notes, proclaiming that not even hell burns hotter than her veins. Blood pounds, nostrils flare, and pupils dilate—until finally the piece climaxes. Dawn breaks, the sun bursts forth, and bells peal out Joy and Gladness.

If someone is bluffing that they're infatuated with Ravel's *Rapsodie Espagnole*, ask if they're familiar with the Real Thing—meaning de Falla's *Nights in the Gardens of Spain*. It's probably de Falla's masterpiece. Stress that no one else has ever captured so perfectly the rhythms, cadences, and melodies of Andalucia (and, head held high, pronounce it with a lisp: Anda-*luthi*a). A murmur ripples across the room: you know what you're talking about.

Bring your bluffing about romantic nationalism to an end with a choice reflection or two about **Jean Sibelius** (1865–1957), who composed a multitude of deeply emotional music for the first thirty years of his life and —without warning—wrote absolutely nothing else for the last thirty years of his life. Ponder *why* . . . Or perhaps you can mock-conduct a few soul-stirring bars from *Finlandia* or *Valse Triste*. To complete the picture of nationalism, especially if you're surrounded by foreigners, never let the topic drop without due tribute to **John Philip Sousa** (1854–1936), without whom there would be no parades or half-time shows.

If the company is, by this time, in its cups, challenge any three to join you in a whistling match of *The Stars and Stripes Forever, Semper Fidelis, El Capitan,* or *The Washington Post* (the march, not the newspaper). From here on, it's smooth marching for any bluffers worth their salt.

The Impressionistic Era (1890–1925)

When you feel you've managed to navigate the waters of romanticism and run the rapids of nationalism, prepare yourself for the murky depths of the next era, which not even Debussy managed too well. **Impressionism** infected hard-core romantics and was rampant for several years, infusing its devotees with dark, soulful emotionalism and passionate outpourings. Mood and atmosphere were *everything*; form lay in the dust. Subjective to a fault, this *-ism* focused on the performer and the cult of color, line, tone, and spirituality.

The Big Daddy of the impressionistic movement (and, some sticklers insist, the only *true* impressionist), **Claude Debussy** (1862–1918), once felt the poison pen of a certain Mr. Krehbiel, a noted American critic who crucified *La Mer* in 1907 with these mortal thrusts:

> Last night's concert began with a lot of impressionistic daubs of color smeared higgledy-piggledy on a tonal palette, with never a thought of form

or purpose except to create new combinations of sounds . . . One thing only was certain . . . that the composer's ocean was a frog-pond, and that some of its denizens had got into the throat of every one of the brass instruments.

The Achilles heel of critics is their commitment to print. Invectives hurled in anger are immutably there to be quoted against them for the rest of their lives. We can choose to believe that Krehbiel was chewing on crow when he later wrote of Debussy's *La Mer* in 1922:

> A poetic work in which Debussy has so wonderfully caught the rhythms and colors of the sea.

But don't you believe it. Odds are that he was hoping nobody would remember his earlier review.

Back to Debussy. Like an impressionistic French painter, he protested the overkill of the romantic school. Heavily influenced by Oriental thought, he expressed the shimmering effects of light on water via tone, chord structure, tricky two-against-three rhythms, and other coloristic details. Subtle and dreamily persuasive, Debussy's *Prelude to the Afternoon of a Faun,* the first of a series of virtuoso compositions, was one of his most successful. *Prelude* is perfect. Say so and *insist* that his most overplayed and worst interpreted masterpiece, *Clair de Lune,* ranks highest as *the* musical cliche. Then score points for praising *Pelléas et Mélisande, Le Martyre de Saint-Sébastien,* and *Fêtes Galantes.* But brush up on your French before attempting these.

If you lack the panache of a *really* skilled bluffer, you

might feel more at home with **Sergei Rachmaninoff** (1873–1943), who distinguished himself by dying in Beverly Hills. He was a gaunt, sad man of Lisztian mold, torn between the fruitful occupation of being a lionized pianist and, at the same time, tending to the humbler duties of being a composer. Rachmaninoff compromised neatly by writing concertos (including No. 2, a favorite in the world's top ten musical War Horses) and playing them better than anyone else ever could.

Critics were always saying Rachmaninoff was finished — but, just as they had *finally* written him off, he wrote *Rhapsody on a Theme of Paganini,* which is the world's best-loved pseudo-concerto (and the background music of a Christopher Reeve movie). Russian authorities asserted that Rachmaninoff's music represented the "decadent attitude of the lower middle classes." How right they were. And as a passing commentary on the music world as a whole, one can't help but feel sorry for Paganini; as a composer he never ranked very high, yet he seemed to supply a lending library of themes for everyone else.

Rachmaninoff's artistry grew second-hand under pupils of Tchaikovsky, Rubinstein, and Liszt. Almost everything he wrote is melodically recognizable, but unnameable. Thus, bluff your way beautifully with oblique references to his *Isle of the Dead, Francesca da Rimini,* or *The Avaricious Knight.* Mention *The Bells* at your own risk.

If you're surrounded by egregious *non-*Americans, who are reverently doing homage to Continental impressionism, cut them down to size with a penetrating commentary on the American impressionist **Edward**

MacDowell (1862–1908), a tonal craftsmen *par excellence.* Rave about his *Woodland Sketches,* particularly "To a Wild Rose," "From an Indian Lodge," and "To a Water Lily." Refuse to retreat an inch on the matter of American prominence in the impressionistic era. You'll discover that no one in the room will know enough about MacDowell to open their mouths, much less phrase a suitable comeback.

The Modern Era (1925-   )

At last you arrive at the epitome of musical expression–the current or **modern era**, which broke so thoroughly with classical form and romantic longings that it often bears little resemblance to music at all. The orchestra, a mere *skeleton* of its former fulsome self, relies on ting-tinglers and hoot-hooters of the most garish tone and timbre. Chord progressions, no longer recognizable by Beethoven's standards, reach into the post-Hiroshima age for *angst* and *sturm und drang.*

Melodically, when the scale was divided into smaller intervals, composers like **Hindemith, Ives, Bartók, Holst**, and **Schoenberg** were cut loose from old moorings and freed to experiment. Today's "classical music" is more a *happening* and less a pleasant diversion. Dissonance reigns. Harmony hasn't the ghost of a chance.

Two composers belong to the transitional era that separates modern music from the previous ilk. The first, **Anton Bruckner** (1824–96), is generally considered a simple man–practically a nature boy, you might gather from some of the critics. If, after listening to one of his symphonies, you still believe he was "simple," then you're *not* the kind of person who should be reading this book. In fact, Bruckner was deep as James Joyce or Simone de Beauvoir, depending on your perspective. He was also an organist, and organists are never simple.

Another misrepresentation of Bruckner is his being bracketed with **Gustav Mahler** (1860–1911). The only thing the two had in common was a liking for long symphonies. Whereas Mahler *really* wanted people to like and enjoy his symphonies, Bruckner couldn't have cared less. In the midst of all the musical money-grubbing going on in Vienna at the end of the nineteenth century, Bruckner quietly enjoyed writing long, unapproachable symphonies and went out of his way to look *un*artistic with close, cropped hair and a spiffy bow tie. Only Tiny Tim has looked less musical.

When Bruckner completed his works, he let anybody play them. A lot of longhaired musicologists were keen to oblige, never having written more than the first eight bars of a long symphony themselves. These rash Wieners, girded with money and influence, got the symphonies played so they could hear their own tinkerings. One should therefore always demand *unadulterated* Bruckner. Never accept a Bruckner symphony unless it bears the label "an Anton Bruckner original" and is full of Bruckner's unmistakable simplicities. The 4th is his "nice" symphony; the rest you can pass over. Bruckner didn't waste time writing pleasant little recommendable pieces. His *Te Deum*, however, is sublime, and it's OK to say so.

Like Bruckner, Mahler had an incurable ambition to write the longest, noisiest, and costliest symphonies in the world (costly because they need so many people to perform them). This epic end he achieved, and it was, not surprisingly, a long time before people could be persuaded to listen to them or impresarios felt like trying to coerce an audience into a Mahler musicale.

Suddenly, however, someone realized that Mahler had *not* written big, long, boring symphonies of the Brahms type which you have to listen to carefully from beginning to end in order not to miss the themes, but had, in fact, simply strung together hundreds of attractive little tunes. It's possible to become comatose during most of his symphonies and still find your way when you come to. You can switch on the car radio when you leave Nutley, New Jersey, hie your way through the Holland Tunnel, arrive in Manhattan and find a parking place with the symphony still going on in a forgetfully energetic manner that suggests it might still be in progress at rush hour.

Almost all conductors get lost during a work like the 7th, which one critic dubbed the "Mad Symphony." No doubt somebody'll prove one day that Mahler *was* psychotic. If not, why did he go to such trouble to write so much when he achieved better results in his short symphonies, like the 1st and 4th? Possibly he was being paid by the bar.

It's said that Mahler had a thing about writing a 9th, but—who knows? He was probably just getting tired of moonlighting while holding down a steady job as a conductor. His chances of leaving an "Unfinished" symphony were thwarted by Deryck Cooke, who polished off the 10th for him.

Today, Mahler suffers from *over*-popularity, but there's still plenty to discuss. Latch on to a fleeting theme in the middle of the 8th and say it reminds you of "Pop Goes the Weasel." Few will rise to the bait.

While you're bluffing about modern music, one of the most "in" people to feign knowledge of is **Erik Satie** (*sah' tee*) (1866–1925). There's also a good chance that you'll genuinely enjoy his music if you buy a cassette or two.

Satie was French and had a lot more fun with his music than most composers do—no anguished Germanic back of the hand to the forehead for him. He'd whip out a little number that was dazzling and call it *Desiccated Embryos*. Or he'd finish an orchestral jewel and whimsically call it *Three Pieces in the Form of a Pear*. No *sturm und drang* here. "We want *our* music," Satie said, "and, if possible, without kraut."

Satie's music is as rash as a child on the last day of school. One is always hearing new musical textures. There's never a sense of the quintessential Satie. He was always evolving, much like Picasso, trying out new forms and harmonies. In his music, one can hear melodies from the French vaudeville era, as well as snippets of American ragtime. He was immensely fond of the ditties that he heard in nightclubs. If you mention his *Sports and Diversions* (an easy title to remember), include this bit of trivia: Satie was offered an enormous sum to write this music—provided that it "sounded like" a series of watercolors. He refused—until he was offered *less* money.

One last thing. There's a strong likelihood that if someone else introduced Satie into the conversation, he (or she) will mention his *Parade*. Pounce on that remark and counter it with "Oh, *that* old tired piece of modern dance debris." Then trivialize your opponent with, "Satie rinsed his wit in *Parade*—but he leavened his *soul* into my favorite, the wonderous *Mass for the Poor.*

If you want to bandy about another modern "name" or two, bring up **Arnold Schoenberg** (1874–1951), one of the most controversial composers of all time. He started out in a normal way by orchestrating operettas, which he did quite well. Then having decided to compose "serious music," he began imitating Wagner and Brahms, but then discovered that Wagner and Brahms had already covered that territory.

After a few lengthy and abortive attempts in the wrong direction, he concluded that he'd have to find a different method. Idly toying with a crossword puzzle one day, he came up with the idea of writing music to a formula that would make inspiration unnecessary. Taking the twelve notes of the chromatic scale in random order, he used each only once. Then he improvised new rules, like playing them backwards or sideways or standing on his head. For the sake of variety, he even cheated and repeated a few.

At first, this method sounded very novel. Schoenberg's "awakening" was instantly taken up by other composers who couldn't write better music than Wagner or Brahms—or even Schoenberg. Since then, twelve-tone music has become the salvation of second-raters and those who lack imagination. It's sad that his scheme for getting away from the limitations of older music produced something that's even more limiting. Its overwhelming characteristic is an inevitable sameness—whoever writes it.

Schoenberg, however, can at least be credited with being the man who did more than anyone else to create a public appetite for old, hackneyed music and an endless demand for piano concertos by Grieg and Tchaikovsky. Even more to his credit, he wrote a book explaining his musical intricacies. A declared liking for Schoenberg will get you ready admiration but will make you few friends. If you *must,* praise his *Verklärte Nacht* or his *Pierrot Lunaire.* Or change the subject to Stravinsky.

Igor Stravinsky (1882–1971) set out to write music that wouldn't be likeable in any way. Purged of all expressions of human emotion, it was simply a logical system of sounds. Through the years he got more and more frustrated by his failure to achieve this peculiar ambition and, to his apparent horror, he even saw some of his early works like *Petrouchka* and *The Firebird* become immensely popular and spoken of with warm affection by ballerinas and nice old ladies.

Driven to extremes by this manifestation of devotion on the part of *part* of the public, he ended up writing works which employed the twelve-tone method, often of about one and three-quarter minutes duration, which were *so* mean and *so* nasty that even some of his greatest admirers have been unable to encore them more than half a dozen times. Yet, Stravinsky is beloved today; he's had a greater influence on twentieth-century music than any other composer. His disciples have written music that's even more off-putting than his own—and have thrived on it.

Mellowing somewhat in his eighties, Stravinsky went around the world conducting and recording his own works superlatively. Accompanied by a faithful Tonto named Robert Craft, he made pointed utterances which Mr. Craft recorded and published in book form. A wise and profitable move for Mr. Craft. Of course, though, Stravinsky was *always* making utterances. He once said that jazz was a "subversive chaos of sound"—and promptly wrote *The Rite of Spring*. Following that, he wrote a number of pieces based on jazz and ragtime. A remarkably innovative man.

Equally mystifying, **Bela Bartók** (1881–1945) is great stuff for people with the mentality that takes naturally to chess, origami, and double acrostics. There's nothing "pleasant" about his compositions, but standing up to them gives one the same exhilarating satisfaction as facing the breakers off Seal Harbor, Maine, or refereeing a hollering match. Indeed, it's been statistically proven that something like 88 percent of the people who actually enjoy reading Solzhenitsyn are also fond of Bartók.

There's no need to look for obscure Bartók, it's *all* obscure. But know these compositions: *Concerto for Orchestra;* the *Music for Strings, Percussion, and Celesta;* and *Sonata for Piano* and your success is assured. Mention the *Kossuth Symphony* and you win the brass ring.

In a tight spot, an easy modern composer to pretend knowledge of is **Gustav Holst** (1872–1934), who's English even though his name doesn't sound like it. Most people have probably heard of *The Planets,* so don't *you* mention it. To shore up your bluffing savvy, especially if you bombed out on Bartók, pontificate on Holst's roots in the "poetic mysticism of the Far East" and touch briefly on his "Sanskrit period." Then *insist* on the importance of his tone poems. If pushed for particulars, cite his *Rig Veda Hymn* and his *Beni Mora.* Then jolt your opponent with a quick reverse and score with the enigmatic term "English lore," singling out his

Egdon Heath, The Perfect Fool, and *At the Boar's Head.*
No one ever survives this crafty deception.

If you really like this particular genre, stick your neck out and praise **Charles Ives** (1874–1954) or **Aram Ilich Khachaturian** (1903–78). Either one – or both – are good bluffing territory in most discussions of music unless you happen to be surrounded by the department heads of Juilliard. For particulars, furrow your brow and refer to the "intricacies" of Ives's *Central Park in the Dark* and to the "heroics" of Khachaturian's *Spartacus.* (Don't even *think* "Sabre Dance.")

At this point, musical bluffing may understandably seem too treacherous to attempt. It isn't. It only *seems* that way. All in all, bluffers – especially male bluffers – are a crazy bunch. They're easily addicted to bluffing; after all, they've been doing it ever since their locker room whopperthon days. They can become almost bluffingly suicidal. They're usually no problem. On the other hand, there's female bluffers, and here, you have to adopt a whole new strategy. Zealous female bluffers never let themselves get *really* cornered. If they're confronted with some smart-ass amateur, they simply unsheath their double-edged tongues and, a few zingers later, they're Queen of the Hill. In bluffing circles, this is common knowledge – so if you're new at the bluffing game, consider yourself forewarned. Don't tease a seasoned female bluffer. As for the males, if you sense that you've hooked a mainliner, go for the jugular.

The "jugular," in any discussion of modern music, is **Alexander Scriabin** (1872–1925). In almost any conversation about modern music, there'll be some coy esthete who'll try to bluffingly overwhelm his listeners with his non-knowledge of Scriabin. Sock it to him. Tell him flat out that Scriabin is an insult to all two-fisted, red-blooded American males. Cite Scriabin's obsession with the left hand: "Who trusts a man who intentionally wrote the most difficult music in the history of the piano for the left hand *only?*" After all, what's the right hand supposed to do while the left one is working triple time, making scythe-like runs and hammering out tremolos on all of the bottom black keys, feverishly attempting to emulate music that's marked "deliriously," "fantastically," and "imperiously"? I mean, what *is* the right hand doing? Buttonhole this twerp. Tell him that you're a devotee of the Lefthanders League, but, in your opinion, Scriabin wasn't using both sides of his brain. Then change the subject to Webern.

Anton von Webern (*vay burn*) (1883–1945) is like that expensive bar of imported chocolate that you squirreled away to scarf down on a cold winter evening when absolutely everything's gone wrong that could go wrong. Use him only in emergencies, and — when you do — *savor* him. There aren't too many bluffers or non-bluffers who can best you at Webern if you remember only a few basics: he earned a Ph.D. in musicology from the University of Vienna (most composers don't have Ph.D.s), and he attempted to escape the worst horrors of World War II by fleeing to Salzburg with his wife, but was shot by a U.S. sentry when he (probably unintentionally) broke curfew. "Ironic," you remark, "considering that he was the *first* to recognize the genius of Charles Ives."

Ives, as we've just noted, is fairly easy pickings for bluffers, so steer the conversation back to Webern. In fact, if you want to sound authentic about Webern, you can own his entire output on four LPs. Give them a listen. If at first they sound strange, remember that most of them have *no key*; an added plus is that the majority of them are less than a minute long. And rarely does he repeat a note once it's left the gate. If you need to plow a few more pertinent Webern phrases into the conversation, comment on his *obsession* for "augmented and perfect fourths and fifths." And then, paraphrasing Schoenberg, remark that in Webern's music, "Every note is a poem, and every chord, a novel." If your listeners seem eager for more, half-whisper, "Webern's music is like seeing a rainbow shatter – and then shower itself onto earth." And then move toward the bar.

If you suddenly find yourself in too deep – outgunned or winnowed out – fall back on a chauvinistic ploy and rally around an American that *everybody* likes – **Aaron Copland** (1900-   ), whose *Fanfare for the Common Man* fosters warm, fuzzy thoughts of Olympic gold medals and flag-waving. Whistle a few lively tunes from *Rodeo, Appalachian Spring,* or *Billy the Kid.* Don't let lesser bluffers think that just because *they* can argue Ives and Satie, you don't have any class.

To round out your discussion of modern music, cultivate terms like "thematic structure," "contemporary sensibilities," and "basic modality." Use these completely at random and find a few special words of your *own* – like "paradigm," "dodekaphonic," and "concatenate." Dip into a book on modern music for additions to your arsenal. Remember *never* indulge in alcohol while using them.

It's impossible for anyone to be prepared for every contingency in a discourse on modern music, but you can always murmur "interesting" or "ingenious" or, better still, utter "ummmmmmmm" noises. Never admit that anyone mentioned is actually avant-garde; instead, suggest that *you* are one step ahead by commenting, "Yes, but perhaps he's a little narrow in his outlook" (or "rigid" or even "predictable"). These terms are difficult to refute.

Just in case you're ever face-to-face with a genuine intellectual, it's dangerous to assert that anyone or anything is derivitive from Stockhausen. Quite possibly, you'll be questioned and *then* where would you be? Better to phrase it ambiguously: "I mean, from where Stockhausen left off . . ." Nobody's likely to know exactly what *that* means.

It'll entail a little work and memorizing, but you should have a few basic words ready to use in connection with some of the prominent, contemporary heroes of the hour. For Stockhausen, for example, "isomorphic"; for John Cage — well, "isomorphic" would be all right there too. The best line of defense if you're bluffing about modern music is to attack. "How can one *generalize?*" you might ask. "Are we to assume some correlation between Babbitt, Musgrave, Glass, *and* Reich?" Smiling, of course, so that your comment can be taken as a joke of some kind. At this point it's best to say, "Hey, your glass is empty. Let me refill it."

A FEW MUSICAL BYWAYS

Musical slumming's a fun game and can be played with finesse by even the most *un*seasoned bluffer. All you need is a fairly simple, commonplace tune that doesn't have very much in its favor nor very much against it, and by constant innuendo, sly nuances, and knowing looks, make people believe that you've found something that they've been unobservant enough to miss. Various breeds of music have become minor art forms via this technique. If the tune can be wrapped in nostalgia—like "Over There" songs or movie themes of the twenties—then you're home free.

Some kinds of music already well-established as cultural byways include these:

Jazz

An early phenomenon in the musical world was jazz, an outgrowth of New Orleans black music, sprung up from generations of gospel, spirituals, blues, work songs, and other forms of lowdown wailing. Jazz started in an obscure way at an unspecified time in American history, and hundreds of books have been written to confuse the issue.

Basically, there's two kinds of jazz:

(1) *Traditional,* where everyone plays together and they all try to outdo each other, and

(2) *Modern,* where each player goes on as if unaware of the existence of the others.

Decide which kind you like and decry the other kind on every occasion; if you can't make up your mind what you like, say that you prefer "mainstream."

Jazz musicians no longer smile or look pleased when they play—a sure sign that jazz is growing up. After all, nobody would expect musicians in a symphony orchestra to look as if they were enjoying themselves. The keynote of your approach to jazz should be deadly serious—the deadlier the better—and, as ever, your language must be chosen like arrows from a quiver. On this topic, though, you can have some fun; nobody in jazz will misunderstand if you say the *opposite* of what you mean. For instance, if you come across a particularly intellectual piece of jazz that might have been written by Schoenberg in a relaxed moment, you could describe it as "crazy." A perfectly good word for a really *good* piece of jazz that meets with your approval is "bad."

If anyone asks you whom you consider the most "underrated" jazz stylist (a favorite conjecture), you might say Ella Fitzgerald or Billie Holiday. Or if they ask you whom you consider the greatest jazzman of all time, you could make quite a reputation for yourself by nominating Charlie Parker, the Beethoven of jazz, the subject of Clint Eastwood's *Bird.* You'll earn your stripes.

Exotica of the jazz world centers less on particular performers or nameable works than on stylistic periods, including Dixieland, ragtime, bop, swing, R&B, and so on. If you get lost on a roll down memory lane, divert your audience with commentary on the "social significance of the movement" and rail against those snobs who reject out of hand the worth of "so dignified a quest." Ponder the evolution of the bongo, sitar, recorder, harmonica, Jew's harp, or tambourine. If all else fails, open the floor to a discussion of the Moog or the non-jazz greats of the modern era.

Country-Western

Songs in this genre are cranked out in the thousands by residents of Nashville and various bedroom communities within driving distance. DJs, VJs, Bible-thumpers, George Bush, and other credible sources have given the stamp of approval to country-western's broad, earthy humor. It now ranks high as good music for overwrought intellectuals, truck driving Muzak for working-class stiffs, and conversational kitsch for literati who want to combat the notion that people who think can't "tell it how it is."

Can you hum along to these classics?

(1) "D-I-V-O-R-C-E"
(2) "Your Cheatin' Heart"
(3) "Happy Trails to You"

Are you well-versed enough to belt out the last verses of the more arcane of Nashville anthems, such as:

(1) "Never Choose Your Wife from a Photograph— It Doesn't Show Round the Back"
(2) "There's a Look in Your Eye That Attracts Me (If Only, My Dear, You Had Two)"
(3) "Will You Take This Wedded Woman to Be Your Lawful Wife?"

A light reading of the biographies of Hank Williams, Tammy Wynette, Merle Haggard, or Dolly Parton will quickly get you into the lingo.

You can do yourself no harm at all (as was once the case) by discussing the merits of rockabilly, which has been written about by learned music critics from the *New York Times* and other respected newspapers and journals. Remember: the great draw of country-western music is its sociological significance and its acceptance as "a serious subject of earnest books and university studies." This is true. *American Men: Bellyachers and Whiners* just might be the title of the next Ph.D. dissertation.

Folk Music

The richest field for the musical slummer is undoubtedly folk music – in its strictest sense, music that no one can be accused of having written. The surest badge to guaranteed bluffing is knowing that the word "traditional" confers the mark of mystery on any piece of folk music. A mere "anon" implies that whoever wrote the piece was thoroughly ashamed of it.

The whole genre goes so far back and is so totally undocumented that anyone can take uninformed guesses at its origins. Folk music in the beginning was simply a series of unintelligible choruses which the guys used to sing together at post-dinosaur-hunt drinking parties. The lead Neanderthal would howl out a note or two, and his compadres would burst into the refrain "With a humph-humph, grunt-grunt, die-die-doo" and then all roll around laughing and have another round of brew.

By the fifteenth century or so, these choruses had advanced as far as "with a fol-de-rol-de-diddle-diddle-dol" and the more sophisticated "with a hey and a ho and a come blow for blow," said to have originated with Robin Hood and his gang of merry greenclads. It was the same throughout the globe with national variations. While "with an oink-oink here and a moo-moo there" was catching on in the colonies and "hey-nonny-nonny-no" was catching on in England, "with a heigh-ho heigh-ho blarney-blarney high-ho" was tops in Ireland and "avec un trala la-la liere-la" could be heard throughout France. Even in distant China, they were at it—"ming ting-wing, pitti-pitti sing-ting" and so on.

After thousands of years, this unending refraining got tedious, and it was then that some anon, slightly brighter than the herd, had the idea for *verses* to link the "fol-de-rol-de-rols." The addition of "As I went out one morning" was then misremembered, misquoted, and improvised on through saloon after saloon clear across the country.

Over in England, the folk song unwound into long, elaborate, and totally fictitious stories along the lines of "The Good Sir Belvedere Rode Out upon his Milk-White Charger" and "Green Grow the Rushes-O," and developed into "Barbara Allen." The colonies continued to keep pace with "When Johnny Comes Marching Home," "Eating Goober Peas," and "Frankie and Johnny."

Any number of public gatherings inspired compositions—public hangings, wrecks of whaling vessels, brawls or clashes with the Establishment, religious revivals, fairs, witch hunts, and lovers' spats. By the eighteenth century, the news of the day was being written down in ballad form and sold on badly printed sheets of cheap paper, some of which survived primitive toilets and have become valued collectors' items today.

In the twentieth century, the interest in folk music really began in earnest. It was then that **Ralph Vaughn Williams** and **Benjamin Britten** in England and **Francis James Child** in the States went around with notebooks in hand (and, occasionally, tape recorders) to capture these old folk songs while there were still singers who could remember them and render them in the proper, tuneless, dismal sort of way.

You can always tell genuine folk singers by the way that they cup a hand around one ear and sing through their noses, thus leaving their mouths free to take a swig of homebrew or share a joint. Another dead give-away is underarm redolence, a sure sign that the singer's got a right to sing the blues by dint of his or her membership in the working class.

Light Music

Those who are acquainted with only less prestigious music-makers might be put off by some of the names so far bandied about in this book. Cheer up! Don't fear. *Don't Worry, Be Happy,* you haven't been left out of the game of musical bluffing. Just bide your time and wait for the right moment. Allow some mouthy, obnoxious fool to rattle on at length about his favorite kind of music or composer, and when it comes your turn to answer " . . . and who is *your* favorite composer?" retort firmly, "Albert W. *Ketelbey*" (*kuh tel' bee*). While they're reeling, add: "Born in Birmingham, England (real name: Anton Vidorensky); studied under Prout. Have you heard his earliest piano sonata? A *great* favorite of

Elgar's. His orchestral music shows a *great* flair for tone color." This little musical trump card can't miss, and all you have to do is bone up on a few insignificant snippets from *A Guide to Popular Music.*

If Ketélbey (very popular in Japan at the moment) isn't your cup of tea, then you might claim Leonard Bernstein, Cole Porter, Jerome Kern, Victor Herbert, or Rodgers and Hart. The likes of Franz Lehar and other Viennese masters, many of whose works sound identically the same, have already established themselves as cult figures. The John Lennon campaign still has some wind left in it, particularly now that his music has been recorded by everybody who's anybody in the rock world. A considerable achievement.

Such lowbrow sophisticates as George and Ira Gershwin, Richard Rodgers, Billy Rose, Sigmund Romberg, and Irving Berlin may have been a little overworked, but if you're quick, you might score points by mentioning Vera Lynn, the Weavers, the Mormon Tabernacle Choir, Nina Simone, the Statler Brothers, or Joan Baez, all neglected songsters at the moment—and all genuine.

If you ever get tired of bluffing it straight, you might consider trying something a little kinky—the so-called bi-bluff. Here, you tell the truth, but you tell it with such over-done, wide-eyed Betty White sincerity that your listener is sure to think that you're bluffing. But you're not. And the more you say and the more fantastic it sounds, the more they'll be absolutely *convinced* that you're bluffing. Later, when they do a little gossiping about a certain "gaffe" you made, they'll be chastened with the truth: you *weren't* bluffing. They were the victim of the infamous bi-bluff.

For example, if someone is belittling American music (compared to European music), stand up straight and tall for America and William Billings. Confess that even you yourself have been lax about not doing more to promote Billings's music — after all, despite his modest reputation, he was our nation's first "professional" composer.

Stifle all protests. Insist that it's so: Billings was born in Boston and was a self-taught tanner (albeit an imperfect tanner, because he couldn't help scribbling scores in chalk all over the tanned hides). Gosh, everyone's heard of Billings's (wink, wink) "fuguing music."

Never heard of William Billings? Draw back in disbelief. Why, he was George Washington's favorite composer; Billings's song "Chester" was sung during the famed Potomac Crossing, and foxholes from Lexington to Concord resounded with selections from all six of Billings's hymn collections. Never heard of William Billings? Why not to know William Billings is not to know one's roots.

America *owes* Billings a revival. It's not enough that the Boston Pops frequently plays "Chester." The entire country needs to honor this fervently nationalistic musical pioneer. And at this point, look off misty-eyed toward the fruited plains, the amber waves of grain, and the purple mountain majesties.

A MUSIC BLUFFER'S GLOSSARY

To talk music, one needn't digest and regurgitate a musical dictionary. Fortunately, you learned a lot of quintessential terminology if, like most of us, you took piano lessons. But if you've forgotten how to begin even the C Major scale, don't give up. Here's a handful of easy terms which every bluffer *should* have some vague understanding of – including the difficult ones that need some explaining and a little understanding of Italian (if you're truly a serious bluffer). We've defined the terms by implication rather than strict meaning, which is the correct bluffer's way to use them.

absolute – Music which doesn't suggest the sound of the sea or leaves rustling in the breeze; it leaves the mind a barren blank and prey to the enjoyment of pure sound. Hence, "absolutely *divine*," "absolutely *dreadful*," etc. For a graphic demonstration, put on George Winter's *Seasons.*

a cappella – An unaccompanied vocal rendition sung by egotistical singers who have no patience with instrumentalists.

accidental – An extraneous note played on purpose.

accompaniment – Soloists believe that it's an obtrusive background to be kept at a low level; accompanists believe that it's a good piece of music ruined by egotistical soloists.

adagio—Slowly and leisurely. The whole point of dragging out each line is to impress the audience with the seriousness of the work. Works presented in the *allegro* tempo never seem serious.

allegro—Quick speed. See above entry and construct your own corollary.

andante—Moderately slow. This comes somewhere between *adagio* and *allegro*. Draw your own conclusions as to the implication.

antiphonal—Music that results when half the choir has been given the wrong music and the conductor allows everyone to have a say in the matter.

arpeggio—A broken chord. Nothing is permanent in this world, not even music.

arrangement—An agreement between the orchestra and the conductor. They'll behave if the conductor'll stop messing around and keep to the music.

atonal—Music written when a composer forgets, or perhaps never knew, what key the piece was written in.

bel canto—The lost art of decorating every other note with your own vocal curlicues.

cadenza—An overlong and unnecessary solo spot in a concerto and used as show-off time. On the piano, the passage is played as fast as possible—as seriously as Glenn Gould or as flamboyantly as Liberace. The term can also be used in everyday situations, as in "She shed a showering cadenza of tears at her first husband's funeral."

cantata—A display of the whole battery—arias, recitatives, instrumental accompaniment, choruses, duets, and sonorous lyrics. Better bring a cushion and plan on sitting for quite a while.

chamber music—Music written for a minuscule number of listeners.

chromatic—Thick-textured music, implicitly romantic, with more notes than can be absorbed by any one person at one time.

classical—The word should *never* be used in the common way, meaning music that needs to be seriously listened to.

coda—An extra bit at the end of a composition, during which people can find their coats and put on their shoes.

coloratura—A singer with an unnaturally high voice and broad *vibrato;* usually her bosom exceeds the sound in vibrations per second.

concerto—The only difference between a symphony and a concerto is that a concerto has an additional player known as the soloist. This makes for an interesting battle, giving both the orchestra and the conductor two adversaries instead of one—rather like a musical wrestling match. With the help of *cadenzas,* the soloist is usually the winner. At the end, the conductor usually graciously concedes defeat and shakes hands.

concertmaster—First violinist of the orchestra; he browbeats the rest of the string players until each of them can imitate the concertmaster's notion of an in-tune A. (Shrinking violets need not apply.)

continuo—A noise like a June bug in a mayonnaise jar, usually made on a harpsichord, which fills up the gaps in baroque music.

contrapuntal—Music with two or three tunes all going on at the same time. Clever music.

crescendo—A gradual increase in sound. The point is to increase intensity without startling casual sleepers into embarrassing themselves with extraneous snorts and mutterings.

diatonic—Music that begins and ends in the same key with only brief and apologetic departures from it. It's *far* better to refer to a composer's "diatonic leanings" than to say that his music is "pleasant."

dynamics—Playing too soft or too loud.

etude—A musical study. These works devote themselves to some aspect of technique, usually for the purpose of raising the performer's worth in the eyes of the musical community.

fingering—The mystique of playing an instrument that critics know nothing about.

forte—(pronounced *for' tay*) The Italian word for "loud" and the opposite of *piano,* or soft. **Bartolommeo di Francisco Cristofori** (1655–1731), inventor of the piano, had difficulty making up his mind and named his original instrument the *pianoforte*.

fugue–A mixed-up composition in which two tunes fight for supremacy. It's no accident that psychologists adopted this term to apply to rather unsettling schizophrenic human behavior.

glissando–A favorite gimmick of amateur male and female pianists with long fingernails who sacrifice their manicures in order to unzip the entire keyboard from one end to the other.

grace notes–Notes thrown in for good measure, with or without grace.

Gregorian chant–A dismally intoned string of religious vowels set to monotonic music and sung in chilled naves by monks in long, brown cowls.

Grove's–The 20-volume Bible of the music world.

harmony–A term of no meaning whatever. Thus, such phrases as "rich harmony," "stark harmony," and "satisfying harmony" can be used indiscriminately.

harmonics–The buzzing sound that stringed instruments can make.

impresario–God-like creatures who "menace" and live in Scarsdale or the environs of Beverly Hills. They dress like well-heeled evangelists or undertakers. Like evangelists, they insist that the world has bilked them of their fair percentage, although they inhabit condos filled with avant garde art, Jacuzzis, waterbeds, and well-groomed borzois.

impressionism–Music that sounds as if it's being played in a thick fog.

improvisation–A term that used to mean a natural accomplishment among jazz musicians; nowadays, it's used only in classical spheres when the music falls off the stand.

intermezzo – Light, fluffy music that makes no pretense of any other motive beyond entertainment.

key – Essential information to have if music is to be discussed with any degree of savoir faire; for example, referring to Tchaikovsky's *Piano Concerto No. 1 in B-flat Minor* is far better than saying, "You know – that piece of his that has 'Tonight We Love' in it."

largo – *Very* slow speed. *cf.* **adagio.**

leitmotif – A piece of music played every time someone makes an appearance in an opera. A good example can be found in the non-operatic but aptly illustrative *Peter and the Wolf.* (A bad example can be found in almost any B movie.)

lento – Another term for slow speed. Musicians seem to like lots of terms that mean the same thing.

lieder – Songs which do *not* have a memorable melody.

madrigal – Medieval barbershop choruses sung outdoors on wet summer evenings.

major – Keys which sound all right.

melody – A word which, like "tune," should *never* be used. "Melodic line" is permissible, but it's better to refer vaguely to "thematic material."

minor – Keys which sound odd or mournful.

modulation – The art of moving from one key to another in a manner that is subtle yet obvious enough to arouse admiration. (Without modulation, there would be no Barry Manilow.)

molto–More of the same.

motet–Choral music sung without accompaniment for a maximum understanding of words in an unknown tongue. A favorite with Bach.

motif–A tiny and irritating tune used *ad nauseam*.

obbligato–An accompanying part which (as the name does *not* suggest) is usually unnecessary and overly decorative.

opus–A code name for a composition, the familiar use of which raises the status of the speaker 100 percent.

ornamentation–The art of making baroque music more interesting (or more tedious, depending on your perspective) by the addition of trills, turns, and so on.

overture–A melody that serves as a kind of "curtain going up" for the entire performance. If none of the tune teasers strikes your fancy, think up a good excuse for leaving early.

pentatonic–Music that can be played on bagpipes, kazoos, or Jew's harps.

perfect pitch–The possession of a sensitive ear that gives one the right to say that performers are off-key.

program music–Music that suggests nice things to think about while it is going on–very popular with the unmusical and therefore included on as many musical programs as possible.

recitative–(pronounced *ray' chi* (also *see*) *tah teev'*) Used when an opera composer has lots of dull words to set to music and admits defeat.

rhapsody—A composition that selects its own style and focus and ignores the rest of the world entirely.

rhythm—The elemental musical sense which critics find lacking in most conductors.

romanticism—Music with themes suitable for use as background for movies or TV films.

rubato—Playing in an old-fashioned and blatantly emotional way

scherzo—A musical joke created by a composer who needed a break from overly serious compositions.

score—(a) Complete copy of the music being played that all the best soloists and conductors like to do without; (b) Complete copy of the music being played that bluffer members of the audience like to have in hand and follow with annoying, miniature flashlights.

segue—To slide one tune into the next one without giving the audience a chance to slither out the door. This is a popular ploy with jazz musicians who split 50-50 with the bartender.

sonata form—A rather complicated formal pattern for the first movement of a symphony painstakingly established by the early composers and assiduously avoided thereafter.

song—A *lied* with a melody.

stopping—A technical term used by string players for fingering. Hence the expression describing a violinist who "doesn't know where to stop."

subject—A trendy term for "tune."

symphony—A piece of music for many performers; it's usually played instead of a concerto when the orchestra can't afford a soloist from out of town.

tarantella—A whirling Italian dance suitable for music halls that are infested with spiders or cockroaches.

theme—A major tune that masquerades in different forms throughout the composition, sometimes played by woodwinds, sometimes by strings, and sometimes by the whole shebang.

timbre—Tone quality; a characteristic which critics dwell on when they can't find a concrete gripe with the performance but insist on a vendetta against the performer.

tonality—A trendy term for "key."

tone poem—A descriptive term for a piece of music that sounds like a sleigh ride, an English hunt, or forest murmurs.

variation—A slight change in a *theme* to let the audience know that the composer was not completely imbecilic and could write more than one line.

vibrato—The minutely wavering quality of a voice or an instrumental sound that critics say most female performers have too much of.

zarzuela—An unimportant term, really, but it does prove that this list covers everything from *absolute* to *zarzuela*.

A MUSIC BLUFFER'S LIBRARY

The average person can remember only so much information. But the bluffer, no average Jason or Jennifer, must give the impression of knowing a great deal more. To fill in the chinks of your repertoire, familiarize yourself with a few **names and works** from each period. If you really want to win points, buy some CDs and learn to recognize the melodies.

Baroque – (1685–1750)

Albinoni (Adagio in G Minor for Strings and Organ)

Bach, Johann Sebastian (Brandenburg Concertos; 2- and 3-Part Inventions; The Passion According to St. Matthew)

Handel (Royal Fireworks Music; Water Music; the Messiah; "Arrival of the Queen of Sheba" from *Solomon*)

Pachelbel (Canon in D for Strings and Basso Continuo)

Scarlatti (Sonatas – 600 (!) of them to choose from)

Vivaldi (The Four Seasons; Gloria in D)

Classical — (1750-1820)

Bach, Carl Phillip Emanuel (Symphony in D)

Gluck (Overture to *Alceste*)

Haydn (The Surprise, Clock, Military, London, and Farewell symphonies; the Creation)

Mozart (Concerto for Piano No. 21 in C [commonly referred to as the *Elvira Madigan* piece]; the Paris, Linz, Prague, and Jupiter symphonies; Eine Kleine Nachtmusik)

Romantic — (1820-1900)

Beethoven (Symphonies No. 3 [Eroica — *not* Erotica], 5, 6, 7, & 9 [Choral]; Fidelio)

Berlioz (Symphonie Fantastique; L'enfance du Christ)

Bizet (Carmen Suite; Symphony in C; L'Arlesienne Suite)

Borodin (In the Steppes of Central Asia; Prince Igor)

Brahms (Academic Festival Overture; Symphony No. 1; Ein Deutsches Requiem; Hungarian Dances; Liebeslieder Waltzes)

Bruch (Concerto for Violin No. 1 in G Minor)

Bruckner (Symphony No. 4, the Romantic)

Chabrier (España Rhapsody for Orchestra)

Chopin (Preludes; Concerto for Piano No. 1 in E Minor; Valse in C-sharp Minor)

Dvorak (No. 9, of course)

Elgar (Enigma Variations; Pomp and Circumstance)

Franck (Variations Symphoniques; Symphony in D Minor)

Grieg (Concerto for Piano and Orchestra in A Minor; Nocturne in C Major; Norwegian Dances; Peer Gynt)

Humperdinck (Hansel and Gretel)

Liszt (Les Préludes; Concerto for Piano and Symphony No. 1 in E-flat; Hungarian Rhapsody No. 2 in C-sharp Minor)

Mendelssohn (Incidental Music from a *Midsummer Night's Dream*; Scotch, Italian, and Reformation symphonies)

Mussorgsky (Night on Bald Mountain; Pictures at an Exhibition)

Offenbach (Gaité Parisienne – the cancan music)

Rimsky-Korsakov (Capriccio Espagnõl; Song of India; Sheherazade)

Rossini (*William Tell* overture)

Paganini (Concerto for Violin & Orchestra in D Major)

Respighi (Pines of Rome; Fountains of Rome)

Saint-Säens (Symphony No. 3 in C Minor, the "Organ")

Schubert (Trout, Little C, and the Unfinished symphonies (7 & 8); Serenade; Mass in G)

Schumann (Rhenish and Spring symphonies; Carnaval)

Sibelius (Symphony No. 1; Finlandia; The Swan of Tuonela; Valse Triste)

Smetana (Ma Vlast; The Moldau; The Bartered Bride)

Sousa (The Stars and Stripes Forever; Under the Double Eagle; Semper Fidelis; El Capitan; The Washington Post)

Strauss, Johann, Jr. (Blue Danube Waltz; Tales from the Vienna Woods; Artist's Life; Pizzicato Polka; The Emperor Waltz; Voices of Spring; Die Fledermaus; The Gypsy Baron)

Strauss, Richard (Also Sprach Zarathustra; Der Rosenkavalier waltzes)

Tchaikovsky (Capriccio Italien; Nutcracker Suite; Symphony No. 6 in B Minor; 1812 Overture; Romeo and Juliet; Sleeping Beauty; Swan Lake)

Vaughn Williams (Fantasia on a Theme by Thomas Tallis; Greensleeves)

Wagner (Der Ring des Nibelungen; *Rienzi* overture)

Impressionistic — (1890–1925)

Debussy (La Mer; Prelude to the Afternoon of a Faun; Clair de Lune)

De Falla (El Amor Brujo; La Vida Breve)

Dukas (The Sorcerer's Apprentice)

MacDowell (Woodland Sketches)

Rachmaninoff (Concerto for Piano and Orchestra No. 2 in C Minor; Rhapsody on a Theme by Paganini)

Ravel (Bolero [subtitled "In Flagrante Delicto" ever since Bo Derek made it famous]; Rapsodie Espagnole)

Modern — (1925–   )

Albeniz (Cantos de España)

Barber (Concerto for Violin and Orchestra; Overture to the *School for Scandal*)

Bernstein (*West Side Story* Suite)

Britten (*Peter Grimes* Sea Interludes; A Ceremony of Carols)

Copland (Appalachian Spring; Billy the Kid; El Salón Mexico; Fanfare for the Common Man; Rodeo)

Fauré (Requiem; Nocturne No. 7 in C-sharp Minor; Sicilienne)

Gershwin (Rhapsody in Blue; An American in Paris)

Granados (Goyescas; Intermezzo)

Holst (The Planets)

Ives (Symphony No. 3–"The Camp Meeting")

Ketélbey (In a Persian Market)

Khachaturian (Sabre Dance)

Lecuona (Malagueña)

Mahler (Symphonies No. 1 & No. 4)

Prokofiev (Peter and the Wolf; Love for Three Oranges)

Rodgers (Victory at Sea)

Shostakovich (Symphony No. 5)

Stravinsky (The Firebird; Petrouchka; The Rite of Spring)